CHIMERA

LEEANN OLIVIER

POETRY

Printed in the United States of America

First Edition
1 2 3 4 5 6 7 8 9

ISBN 978-1-949540-63-5

Cover art "So this is how" from Jules Verne's novel Around the Moon, drawn by Emile-Antoine Bayard and Alphonse de Neuville, 1872

Steel Toe Books
steeltoebooks.com

For special discounted bulk purchases, please contact sales@steeltoebooks.com

CHIMERA

TABLE OF CONTENTS

CHI.ME.RA
/ky-meer-uh/
noun

1. (in Greek mythology) a fire-breathing female monster with a lion's head, a goat's body, and a serpent's tail.
2. a strange, horrible, or impossible idea or figment of the imagination.
3. (in biology) a person who has cells from two different sources, such as a solid organ recipient.

I

They Ask Why You Don't Just Leave

Because your lungs are heavy as deadwood
and your eyelids wax and wane, words caught

in your teeth like a dark art, a snake plant,
your tongue a huddle of feathers. The monster

collared, you sleep the sleep of the dreamless,
a triquetra of wolves curled around your shins.

But monsters have a way of shifting shapes
and crawling in. This time he carries a hooked

blade, the tips of his tree fingers flamed
into kindling. You follow, hollow as a vertebrate's

husk, his horseflies hemming you in, their static
a wild cackle. Because instead you carve and cleave

through gnarled weeds, a claw-footed tub upturned
at the cusp of the forest, Orion's lullaby a tendril

seeping life into your sleeping veins, your silhouette
backlit between the birch skeins, your heart a red

thread spooling. Because you'll outlive this wintering.
And holy folk will sing over his bones while the cold

sea swallows everything wave after wave after wave.

Mute

In the bedlam of the liver ward the poisons
seep upstream. My neighbor, snake-mean,
curses in Spanish, *pendejo*, when they ask for
her name, my own throat ghosted into
a phantom, an owl song, a burial at sea. Bare
backed blizzards flutter behind my eyelids,
a giantess glued together inside my boiled gut

bred of hushed whispers. The woodcutter
unsnarls my copper veins, botanical as cattails
while slats strap me to the bed and shadow
puppets sprawl into supernovas on the walls,
my mind a tinderbox of unsent letters. I'm a splendid
shut-in. Beneath my tongue white egrets walk
a tightrope and I grapple like an animal for language.

after Ezra Sun

Storm Shelter

after the storm
your body

becomes bunker
to pandemonium

your heart
a nuclear winter

you heave open
your ribs' hull

creatures clamber in
cramped and chittering

fur and tooth
squirm and blight

your couplings
little apocalypses

they eat at you
healer turns monster

bright spinal knurls
spatter against the wall

a Pollock painting
your gut a panoply

pagan knot
bed of snakes

Medusa wound
Medea mad

you name yourself
Aftermath

Origin Story

Eleven malevolent wolves silver
the dark, gifting gooseflesh, your radiant
bones croon, a changeling thing, a buckskin
blacktop zippered with stitches. David Byrne
sings sex and sin, sax and violins, still the world
keeps its spin. You wriggle out of the sundress

of your skin like a ribbonfish. Listen. A mess
of dresses rustles in your mother's attic, hems
hissing. In the pit of your chest a lock unclicks,
star whorls orbit in a glass carousel. Medics
circle your gurney, a pilgrimage, their
human ocean slaps and slithers, spilled

mercury squealing into milky bowls. The jut
of your wing bones knots indigo, rumbling
gulls gouge and purge, your tongue too swollen
to shut your mouth, your throat too swollen
to scream. You wrest your broken body from
this bed, clutching its jigsaw wounds, wearing

antlers instead of pearls, the ripples of a black
moon lapping. You're swathed in leather
like a stingray, draped in orchid bulbs that daze
and bewile. Gravity fevers you through the wild
wood from maiden to crone, the second act
snuffed by rough male fingers, dragging

your jagged slander where the sweetgrass
and sourgum sandpaper your calves. Hoof
and paw, stalk and woodsmoke, a blight
of whitened sycamores, smokestack fumes
flicker and flail. You hunker in the makeshift
crawlspace, riddled with rot. Rain rattles

on the roof like a metal grate over a storefront
until urban memories dim, until all you are
is bristle and brim. Only witches live
in the woods. They thrum with want
and willow shiver. After the storm they
hush your howls. After the storm you are free.

Hungry Ghost

Manta rays wrangle
in tanks of ink, spider-webbed
ghost crabs scrape the night-

scented street. The sea
this evening washes maps of
germplasm on her

banks. Intravenous
pumps beep and sputter, the glut
of white noise plunging

me underwater
where feral muses warble
over parasite

flights of lionfish.
Maybe the sea keeps me hunched
and feral gnawing

on roots and bark in
a dark crook of her dream as
I croon for all I

might lose. Memories
tangle in her coral,
Titian-red, teeming

with weeds that flay me
as I try to wade home. I
will not drink from the

stream of Lethe, its bite
like ink cut with salt. Outside
the ICU sky-

light's frosted splinter,
the moon stalks nervy as an
onion. I chase

my pulse like a bone-
hungry ghost, my lungs purpled
over with drowning.

The Girl Without Hands

Open, love, open. The Keepers incant and ring
around my hospital bed, caroling glam craft,
offering tiger's eye, rose quartz. My nephew slips

a slim column of gypsum into my palm and reads
The Outsiders aloud, chanting the sacred Trinity:
Pony, Johnny, Cherry. In the space between sleeping

and waking, autumn ticks over to winter, a shiny dime
flipped tailside. These are the spells that bind.
On the news someone's been loosening animals

from the Dallas zoo, leopards slinking through
the metro, monkeys crouched in a makeshift cage,
a lion prowling the side of I-35, leviathan,

his fallow cowl a wheat-field surging under
the Texas sun, honeyed as a vial of cadmium lemon.
My body tethered to a devil's nest of tubes and wires,

I wait for my silver hands to grow like moon mirrors,
molding the whole of dreambeds in brain caves
from cobwebs and clay, mute words crowding

my mouth like minnows while the Keepers keep
watch. They speak for me when I've cut out
my tongue, and when I've lost my hands, they pray.

Under the Tongue

The wine god spits words faster than I can catch
them and string them up like cherries or pills.
They spill down my back fat as slabs of rare
meat while the LP crackles and *the tap drips*
under the striplight. The sun god pecks

through the wreckage like a black vulture
or a homicide detective plucking landfill petals
to laurel the dead: they love me, they love me not.
The first time I see my tumor on screen, a smudge
of dark smoke, a sleeping snake, it names itself

Malignant, but before Dionysius can whisper a new
lexicon in my swelling brain: encephalopathy,
meld score, hepatic coma, the gods flee like ghosts,
their lyrics tossed in a cauldron, Apollo unable
to arrange language around my gurney in a tarot

spread: the hermit, the chariot, the seven of wands.
But the Keepers came before gods made language,
yowling, sublingual, scrawling my star chart on
ICU walls in great swatches of ochre and lapis,
mapping me back to Plath's chant of the heart:
I am, I am, I am.

Kindred

In the hospital
you hold vigil, my touchstone,
though my swollen brain

distorts your features,
bulges your big eyes into
cinder goggles, roses

inked on your skin snaking
around the white room. But I remember
you beardless, your hair

a shock of obsidian.
Two decades click and whir back-
ward, silver as

mechanical owls,
to the times we'd spill like spools
of silk into the

coming dark when X
was our only pronoun, our
friends shot up with back-

alley estrogen,
punks pulsing past the streetlamps,
mapless in our tatted

sleeves, the weather a
birdless sky, a soundtrack of
sirens dazzling,

syllabic. We furnished
our first apartment with props
from the theatre

dumpster, a tapestry

of thrones and skulls rattling inside
the slapdash cathedral

we called home. We'd drag
back, clutching our treasures like
bags of ashes, our

trauma bond a quantum
entanglement. Sometimes our
strangelove was beastly

but at least it was bright,
at least you could see it from
Venus. Even now

in the lunar sea
of my cerebellum, our
bloods' thrum hitches us

tight, our ligature
a lodestar, a gold tooth glinting
in the mouth of the night.

Ribbon the Dark

I remember that winter the river
from lover to beloved ran over

with blood, encircling my ankles
as I slogged through its springs.

I remember the rare snow silvered
your bluebeard black, your blackbeard

blue, shaken loose from your gleaming
whiskers. I remember the glimmer

of gunmetal eyes and quicksilver
limbs, your whispers grizzling my skin.

I remember the hunter encased in gold
armor, his ochre no match for your

chrome, your white teeth nicking
the folds of my cloak as I cut out

my heart, a sweetmeat in a basket.

Ritual

The dead wear moss wings, ringed
in whispers, the fabric of your skin
taut as a secondhand dress. Locusts
hum like madhouse lodgers speaking
in tongues, embers of fire and brim-

stone briars smoldering. You're a pilgrim
in the god's damned world where vapors pierce
the pines' lungs, the dark devouring
your dream-enclosed disguise in a duet
of hammers and drums. Over ravenous

caverns and wine caves, fat bright stars
graze like a gang of harbingers, an obstinacy
of bison hunched along the water, horns
and hooves haunting the badlands, bell,
book, and candle. Hell, hook, and idol,

his sepia lips plucking the pipes
of your spine like piano keys. He lassos
your bones like a shaman, a raptor
whose grammar feathers and plumes,
his birthmark barbed wire along his collar-

bone. Sometimes the innocent are bound
to the damned. All your bodies buckle,
your heart an unrung bell, the buck moon
white-knuckled, low and swollen like a tooth-
ache. The dead dream deeper still.

Spindle, My Spindle

I'm a lotus eater, a bon vivant. Sick
with want, *the quiet velvet cult of it,*
I tap the rosaries of your vowels one
by one, cosseted in the honeyed vellum

of your Southern tongue, your letters
gossamer, the silken seam that holds
my spine in place. But I'm keen to learn
your palms' gravel, the muslin of your neck

where I'll coil, dreaming cities from your
flesh, your jugular my equator. Debased
to cur, I'll gnaw at you for seven minutes
on a squalid pier, knowing you by the dark map

of your eyes, a mating dance of cranes. Lake
Charles is the grayest world, its skies sheets
of poplin dipped in pewter. How I ache, navigating
this verbal labyrinth, to weave of our skin one skein.

after Lucie Brock-Broido

Persephone in Texas

These years I've crawled to the mouth
of the cave while the long dancers
bowed to black, but I'm remembering
how to woo them back, to whip my life
into star instead of stone. Underground
pomegranates purpled my lips, my eyes
like an oil spill, hair a river of blood
dripping down my back in a flood so black
it could stain the cavern, your dark heart
swelling in me like a sea-star spreading
its fingers, my stomach a fractal lampburst,
an electric roadmap lighting up my veins.
Now I belly up to a warm patch of earth,
bare feet seething on hot asphalt, brisk wind
like quick moths pecking my face, and I know
this is the season of madness, spring teeming
like bright bones aboveground. Now I can bask
in the sun for hours, my hair your wheat, my back
your leather lap, come lie, Hades, the grass
smells of flesh. The moon grunts with envy.

Belly of the Beast

Above the pit of the stairwell I watched
my father and his militia, men with brass

wings peppering their uniforms like monarchs,
women with feathered hair and eyelashes

like spiders. Their tongues and bodies
loosened as they drank. I smelled the tang

of gin, heard the clink of ice in tumblers,
the plunk of green olives smooth as emeralds.

My father taught me how to mix martinis, roll
cold onions around on my tongue, slam

back vodka with ice. My father never taught me
how to swim, to read or dance or fish. But I

can do all of those things. My father bound
me in blood to the women before him, Creole

chimeras with a claw in each world. Carnivore
that I was, I watched my father drink his supper,

waiting out his indifference like a tigress,
haunches hunched, sedate but impatient for meat.

Contraband

It wasn't an attic but a Winnebago in Shreveport
where my grandmother Annie kept
her secrets, a stack of paperbacks stashed
in a grocery sack under the narrow bed.

I'd huddle there thumbing the pages,
a heathen hunkered down, my heartbeat
a rabbit in the hushed trailer, my brain
an unspooled skein as the hues

of Cleo Virginia's underworld hummed
over me. I built an altar there, each
afternoon after school a vigil, a fairy
ring of pop tops, sparrow feathers

for safekeeping, mint-condition moth
wings, dead from natural causes, hauled
solemnly in a flat, black box. I could
unloose the die-cut characters on the cover, a cult

of Dresden dolls shuttered in thorns,
their haunted faces peering out, pale
as milk. Meanwhile in his mother's purse,
my soon-to-be best friend found a boy

who shined like he did, shimmering
into meaning from inside a maze
of craven pages. However we come
to reading, we become readers. We see

our own weird hearts mirrored
in pulp, and the earth is a safe
cracked open, her secrets like attic
flowers creeping into the sky.

Save Me From What I Want

On my brother's couch in Brooklyn, lulled by the Q
Train's whir and the conductor's bright monotone: *Next stop*
Coney Island, I dream of a turtle, thirteen scutes spiraling
across her callused carapace, one for each new
moon of the year. I lug her to safety, pivoting the broad
disk of her back around like a ship's helm until her tail
turns toward me, but she shimmies out of her casing
like a burlesque dancer, and I catch her glass-green
belly in my hands. The man down South I am scared to want
says we only dream of mirrors, our psyches split across
each creature we encounter, my aquatic shadow either
anchoring her armor tight or slithering out of it, chewing
through nets, learning to love even what swims too close.

Ostara

Night calls unbreakable wild girls
and beasts, spooky green-screen
graffiti, a resurrection. You love
the white moon circles and purple

halos, dogs going prophet, paradise-blue
heartbeat raining alien music, orchestras
and choruses. You whistle essential shots
in the dark when the fog of the riverbank

rises like a holy ghost and April evenings
come with no memory. Then night moves
like a flower, all daisy face and fairy blossom.
Or a star. There is a kind of power in that,

a testimony, a witnessing. Spring storms grizzle
the high mother planet. You decide what's sacred.
You don't have to be here. Plush wild dogs wrap
tiny truths, adrift on a wide, unpunctuated sea,

asterisks and little barnacles, bottomless apothecaries.
This dis-ease is a black art, its jazzed badlands
wading and flawed. Every secret you tell
makes telling the next one easier, the forest

still drips albatross guts and hope clawed as hunger.
Buddha said in this life we look for our fingerprints
from other lives, risk diving full hell. In Hindu
mythology Kali is the goddess of time and change,

of power and destruction. She could easily
you think be the goddess of now. Brooklyn streets
are slick and wet, the pavement disappearing
under iridescent puddles, the sky closing in. It begins.

David Bowie Is

In April New York skies are sheets of poplin dipped
in pewter. Acid rain casts a purple sheen on trash bags
skirting the streets, plastic flashing wet as grackles.

They sparkle like falling stars, so I make a wish anyway
and slip inside the Brooklyn Museum, its house of mirrors,
catacombs sprawled out like maps of fungi bubbling

underground. Here I'm a specter creeping through
the Starman's cerebral sparks, headset caging my brain
in glamour. I left you in Texas to thrash and flail. I left you

in Texas to slip and wail in your own spilled guts, your
animalian anger a caterwaul, a yowl, an ultraviolet
noise that ripped my ribs apart, your fist of love

a hammer above my head. Grief inflates, a lead
balloon in my chest, my limbs liquid metal melting
into the gallery floor. But David Bowie is Lazarus,

is Lucifer, his left eye the horned moon of a black star
I want to bask in. I'm a speck of space debris dancing
in his velvet vacuum, vespertine and reverent. I'm a

dilettante, a cosmonaut piloting his planet, resurrecting
the spectrum where he saunters and furs, his right eye
earthshine shivering down upon me like the chrome

of a quiet sun, his baritone a crossbreed of croon and snarl
coaxing your poison from my lungs, his flowing coats cinched
in to a wasp waist, leotards lean as cats. David Bowie is

mending the splits in my psyche. *You love me, you love me*
not. You're a beast in yogi's clothing. On the day of your
execution women will kneel and smile. I left you in Texas

to burn and keen, I left you in Texas to cackle and crow.
David Bowie is teaching me that everything changes. Like
the old gods, he is showing me my ship knows where to go.

Martial Art

An olive in a fifth of gin. An airman

in an armored vest. A Cajun

with his olive skin. The maiming

made manifest. His cropped hair

thick and black as sin. A killer

with no crimes confessed. A fishnet

filled with blackfin bass. A bayou

steeped in deep Terrebonne. A trumpet

in its clutch of brass. A great ghost

he could not outrun. A closed fist

through a pane of glass. A daughter

and the damage done.

II

Bolivar Ferry

As we cross over the water, moon jellies
clap the causeway, filmy, phosphorescent,
Bolivar a black pearl of a bayou. I swear

I can smell the specters skimming the seawall
and grazing planks of abandoned factories,
Gulf air so glutted with ghosts our tongues

turn gray. Dune plants plume like undines
in the lagoon and a tangle of tanzanite nets
dangle from the mosquito fleets. We watch rapt

as red-tailed hawks rim the swampland, a black-
necked stilt cranes its bill, stalking the marsh
and a yellow-crowned night heron screams,

the queen of the sea. Here the levels rise
like ancient water serpents, higher and faster
than any port on earth, loop currents surging

warm water deep into the Gulf's green arms.
Under-bellies of sand-dwelling sanderlings
glimmer in the seagrass where nettles swarm, this sin

city a symphony of tentacles and triple-digit
heat, turbulent whitecaps more sulphur than azure,
rich with gypsum and ocean jasper. In twenty

years She could be submerged, all the wraiths
from the Great Storm doomed to keep swimming.
But for now shorewinds whip white horses lush

on the water's edge and sea-rose oleanders overlay
the inlet in a lunatic fringe. Broadway still shivers
down the spine of the island where Bettie's brass-

bound souvenir box locks itself, clutching her secrets
like a prayer shawl, the ghosts of Galveston little
hat tricks rattling our brackish bones loose.

Hurricane Season

My Creole ancestors had languid names
like Aurelia and Delphine. The swamp sang
in their veins as green as rivers. I dream
the night before the Great Storm, the sisters creep
to the edge of the pier, dip their nets and wait
for meat, two egrets in a tangle of vines, the moon-
light like bangles on their wrists, and after dawn
the sun's drone turns the moor to loam, violet
skimming the gulf in a skirt of crushed orchids.
The girls sprawl on the front porch, watching the sky
glower and sink, darkening to plum, watching
the vultures wheel and dive as black angels,
Apollo's Aurelia immune to the glum omen,
content to wile her days, to wait and watch
and shimmer under the flambeau of the bayou,
luminous and futile, a mermaid drying her scales
in the sun. But Delphine prays to a different
god, limbs aquiver, she dances like a dervish
while the sea swells, later learning whom to love
when she sees what crawls from the shambles.

True Crime

Violent love-drugs knuckle the peeled world
in an intimate alien cinema. I'm a housebound
sea dweller stuck virtually searching: uncrowded
beaches, witch hunts, tattoos, manslaughter. Before
the storm I drove South all night, past a brothel
called the Moonlite, to taste Memphis pure wildflower
honey, its beekeepers hanging green manuscripts
to smoke out the queen in a wild forest exodus.
In a dream I wrote this poem: "Apocalypse Camp
at the Dawn of the Great Extinction." Spellbound
on a doom loop wonderland, I stumbled farther
South to Fontainebleau Beach, guzzling sea
salt chards, black krill, opalescent swirls in pigments
pomegranate, only darker, like a plague of unsolved
femicides. White nighthawks silvered the most remote
ocean, its helium escape valve a bauble star ring
as perpetual light became shadow,
and I knew then I'd be yours forever.

2004

I remember how much we watched
the stars in our pre-screen silence,
spotting sister sigils like Scorpius
and Taurean, bright bodies emerging
from the skyline. We whirled into spirals,
the songs from our lungs dark. Moon
after moon, we twisted ourselves
into eclipses, animal hearts shuttered,
our bones cages, on the hood of your old
Honda civic, candy-apple paint scraped
and blanched pink from years under
the Southern sun. Hundreds of miles
from any shoreline we needed to untangle
the sky's mosaics. We needed to come
undone in the spaces between the rain
hours, a dirge of dappled patterns reeling
above the roller rink. We'd blot out
our roots, Cajun and Caddo, a slew
of bad fathers, furled fists and flasks
inked with cheap whiskey, until their absence
was nothing. When George W. was the worst
villain we could fathom, we'd roadtrip
to D.C. with our slapdash signs like ragged
flags, your lion's mane growing longer
every year, shot through with red-gold
from your mother's Irish blood. I'm almost
glad you didn't live to see the green
world unbraided into pixels and monsters
big as quarries lumbering in broad light.

after A.E. Stallings

Brood 22

All summer the magicicadas sputter and scrim,
a whispered chorus chirring like wire brushes

on snare drums. This Baton-Rouge brood of stragglers
rises four years early from their subterranean chambers,

jolted out of cycle by the over-warm soil. Hatchlings
bunch in branches, cloaking themselves in exoskeletons

to emerge immortal, imago, feeding on the xylem fizz
of root sap and molting into winged things.

Let their tymbals throb, a squeeze box of ribs
buckling one after another in a glamorous babble.

The Keepers and I spill onto the balcony, marveling
at the sea of sound, the caterwauling of a million cats,

the mating dance of an alien race, the lament of jilted
lovers doomed to sing their throats out, to rasp and dance

and clamor until the room is all on fire, red-eyed
and green-skinned, wings as membranous as embryos.

Let us from our safe distance hear them shrilling
the word *pharaoh* over and over on a loop like a prayer.

Enthralled by their frenzy, let us choose the fugues
that might drag us from the deep. Let the Pretenders

hijack my world, flying into the house like pigeons
from hell. But half a year later, let it be Stevie who delivers

me from my hospital bed with her cicatrix of black
skirts, veined wings reverberating through the ash

trees, limpid as vapors. Let the brood report back to the Muses:
This is the season she emerges. This is the year she's reborn.

Malachite

Your love affair with the sun will end
are the last words the transplant
nurse utters like a sorceress,
her warning the color of a gangrene
sky just before a tornado winnows
into spirals. What about the green,
I think, though I haven't seen
it in weeks, sleet gnashing at the ICU
window's gray sliver. But the green
finds me in six months' time, slipping
from stillness to the Pineywoods,
all the greens of June hum-strumming
my summer skin, sleek as shot silk,
a mackerel sky stippled calico
kaleidoscoping, a chrysalis glinting
in the glancing light where envy
zinnias and wildcap wildflowers ribbon
the rose-mallow grass, jeweled geckos
gild the blackjack oaks and violet-green
swallows swagger along the broomsedge.
And yes, my new flesh pinks
and mottles, my inner coil a kettle
bubbling over, cooking from within
as sure as our doomed mother planet,
but for now I am green again, a chimera
with luna-moth wings, my donor's
bluestem wild-boy cells slicking
the ribbons in my bloodmap
like a mossgod. What the nurse forgot:
young galaxies glow green before they spill
stars and sugar scarabs scuttle over the hearts
of pharaohs, green as longing unveiled.

Midsummer, Oregon Coast

That first summer after the storm my boiling
body urges my love and me to higher ground where gods

and monsters merge at the edge of the world
in folds of terrible velvet. Here verdant vegetation yawns

with yarrows and blueblossoms, Pacific bleeding-heart
plants a slash of crimson in a sea of green. Bigfoot brinks

the border between man and animal, a megafauna
urging us into the wild. Whales slither like giant sea

serpents, barnacles speckling their slick mammalian
skin. We gasp to see Scarback surface, a resident gray

with a manmade gash fishtailing her silver middle. I'm lost
in folklore. Douglas firs and Western hemlocks weep green

rivulets, the forest floor all felt and fallow, her under-
story lush with moss. But human mutations drag me back

to my small, flawed body, my scar salmon and jagged
like the wounded whale's, a cocktail of meds every twelve

hours to keep my immune system from striking
the strange liver alive in my abdomen. The Chinook

peoples call this place and its creatures *skookum*: survivor,
leviathan, behemoth, now fighting tooth and claw to adapt

to greenhouse gases. Waves decapitate trees
in the phantom forest, relics of towering Sitka spruces

arranged in a pagan ring cairn, Satan's cauldron an ancient
siltstone sea cave, a swirling churn as waves fill the rocky

bowl like a witch's brew. I'm a monster too, a chimera,
DNA doubling in my blood, lion-hearted and bull-headed,

the body of a snake. But in this sorcerous landscape
I'm neither goddess nor beast. I dangle my feet off the lip

of the crag, whales blow and waves lap and loom, foam-white.
For the first time I know in my bones myself on a map,

a speck of dust pinned on the border between giant swathes
of emerald and azure, aware my erasure would be effortless,

still I'm hanging on tight, a skookum fighting like hell's
phoenix for my one wild and precious life.

variation on a theme by Mary Oliver

Mercury

All summer we basked like lizards for a break
in the weather, a scourge of grown grasshoppers
gnawing away the green until we languished

in a yellow hellscape, dull as the bald eye Poe's
narrator buried under the floorboards. Heads bowed,
we whispered to September, a liminal pearl,

a between-worlds traveler, mercury-cytochrome
silent, ghost-gray and wolfish, her skies a sight-
hound, the tarnished topcoat of a copper-bellied

water snake. This morning as I cross the bridge
to the transplant clinic, dove-gray drizzle coats
the world in smoked glass, and my windshield

mirrors my insides, rain marbling the pane. A gray-
crowned crane dive-bombs the cloudburst
above the river. In nine months I've rebirthed

myself into a Virgo, virgin liver, my still slender
body a magick trick, pewter roots mottling my black-
cherry hair, a sign of trauma telltale as my hockey-

stick incision. My sick time all used up, I juggle
the fourth week of fall classes to meet this mile-
stone. I'm a secret keeper, a tightrope walker, tip-

toeing through the rubble of our gutted campus,
buffered by the fierce grace of my students
and allies. One autumn before the sickness my sisters

and I flew to New England, graveyards and ghost-
hunts, crisp leaves dazzling the dappled planet
like flames. But back in Texas, fall's whole tableau

smolders chrome, a flock of whisky jacks, tricksters
quaking in the birch trees, gloom-filled but glinting,
moonstone, hawk's eye, mother of the bride. No golds

or glamours here, no flicks of Titian or henna. Still
there is beauty in the in-between, its silver queen,
its gunmetal and globe thistle. Our relief

from relentless heat a rain-dance mizzling the parched
crops of our Southern hearts, all oyster, ash,
and aluminum. Let us revel in this limbo. Let us laud it.

Polaroids

Grainy and sun-spotted, first the curve
of your back a quick shadow, then dusk,
then parasite sky of no color, each flecked
spindle splitting a terrible sea of dead stars.
Something thundered from the wreckage,
a great black scavenger brooding above
us, hushed and holy, the plastic clack of beetle-
backs in the grassland below. That night
we snuck to the Sabine River to bury ourselves
in water's green skin, September's teeth
silvering our gills while Michael Stipe sang
nightswimming deserves a quiet night.
In the water my body tethered then untethered,
my body your canvas, jewel-winged, my body
reverent, revenant, one vertebrae at a time,
instead of a circus freak or a carnival mirror,
instead of a glass figurine. We marooned
like minnows, brutal mutations, yarrow
yowling along the banks, your hands
in my ribbon-black hair. Now what do I have
left but relics arranged in an ancient grid?
What have I birthed but a language of scars?

Trail Turns Cold

With devils' knots and netherworlds, I've tried
to raise the dead. I've creatured the creeks' secrets
with dream needles, needing to weed your regalia

from the rubble, to puzzle out the patchwork
of your disappearance, fearing your lake-dark
eyes plucked out like olives. Once I took your old

Cure t-shirt to a Dia de Muertos festival, folding
it into a nicho box like a prayer. Now it drawls, a relic
in my closet, cotton so frayed it's almost translucent.

Something warm and ragged unravels itself
and coils blindly like a claw around the other end
of this bright hunger. In a violet hour, our want

was thick with salt and skin, bow to violin, violent
but orchestral, you the cradle that lulled my fevered
head. Night bred your fingers urgent as laurels

down my ribs, our wine-dark world a satin hiss,
your fevered letters a gospel now tossed into a box
with news clippings trumpeting *Trail turns cold*

in search for missing college student. I know I'm not
Diana; still a quiver of arrows brims my hipbone,
a mandolin's morse code prodding me to catalogue

your scars' cartography, your vanishing act a looped
track of blue so endless it eats its own tail. First love
is a splitting of self, a theft of who we were before

we slid ashore. Over and over October tongues
reconstruct the hunter's moon, the past a beast
in hiding from the stars.

Spellcraft

A trail of breadcrumbs ferries
from my door, brother, conjuring

you back to me, back through the black
forest. What alchemy can I work to shake

you, rattle your bone-bleached cage, spook
the ghosts that harangue, their tongues

waggling an augury of gloom? The truth
is, Hansel, I've escaped the witch, but you

still dwell in her candied hellhouse,
its bitter sweets looming like suns.

And my magicks pale, mawkish matched
with her wildwood, mad-eyed ways, her

hoodoo brews that bedevil and doom.
How will I know you still, all glutted

and ripe, all keen for the kill, your fat
heart trembling in her hands like a lark?

And what am I without you, brother—
scant, twinless, a halved apple bruised

blue and turning to rot? I call you back
to me, back through the black forest.

All Hallows

Enter, October, drizzle down
the xylophones of our bones

and cloak us all in your
magicks. Hang your honey-

comb moon upside
down in the sky, bells

buzzing, boots click-clacking
on wet asphalt. Whisper

your laments. Uncrown
the scream queens of summer

and rise, red-haired, resplendent.
Bend spoons and bedevil our exes.

Heather us with the rust
of hearts you flick and fizzle

like fireflies. Shake the sugar
maples until their russet

leaves quiver like preachers
at a tent revival and conjure

our ashen tongues clean.

Psyche

Half of her gods are sun-drenched, pale-
haired angels with eyes like bruises, too elusive
to pluck and pin to her breast, strange baubles
of amethyst and agate. The other half
are cave-bound hunters with blood-
rich mouths, ribbons of damned souls slicing
between their calves like quick black
snakes. Eros alone eludes. And it is not
enough to see him sleep, to see him heathered
in robes of limp light. Women devour. Women
want viscera, marrow. She dreams she lives inside
his head, her limbs dangling from his sockets
like rubies. She can run her tongue's honeyed tip
along his brain trenches and quell the angry
hints that glint and crouch there like tin soldiers.
When he squirms beneath her flame, his long
lambent form lights up like a torched witch,
gleams like an eel, drags fingers of dusk down
her cheeks until she is the one bathed in shadow.
Still it is not enough, the chant of acid rain
on his luminescent ribs. Eros awakes enraged
and tells her it isn't her job to crawl inside.
She was made, instead, to be invaded.

Shadow Work

In fairy tales the women weave, the women spin
until fingers bleed, our legacy to mend the rips

that halve us. Louise and her *maman* tended linens
on the banks of the Bievre River where papa planted

poplars, and the water, later paved over, wove
like wool thread through everything. Lemon-bright

spots and stripes on ink, eight legs sprawled in goddess
pose, in October the orb weaver lays her last clutch

of eggs. Spiderlings hatch crawl stagger swagger
lilt and pitch. Maman ensnares honeyeaters in tombs

of silk and weaves worlds from the backs of black
sheep, a diva rebuilding her web at dusk with rhythmic

rocking and *rentrayage*: reweaving across the cut. Orb
weaver shows us our nature as creators, shows us

the filaments that glint through tall grasses, stitching
us all into a cosmology of stars. In fairy tales the women

weave, warp weft spindle spiral loom and scroll.
Weaving is the only way we know to make things

whole. Like Louise and the weavers, I gather the bombed-
out bits of my life and ravel them into tapestries.

What else is there to do with all these needles
but work them to weave words from bloodied thread?

after Louise Bourgeois, French-American artist

Remedy

Caddo Lake creeps across the border
between Louisiana and Texas, dragon-
shaped, a flush of musseled pearls. A seam
bisecting water and sand, a wonderland
where found-folk slip to disappear.

On the go-devil boat our guide Remy prays
for a hard winter to kill salvinia invading
the scrim in a plague of green. His fingers
weave a garland of waterlilies and beauty-
berries, dried lotus pods big as fists.

Behind the backwater boathouse a swamp
rabbit skitters, bald cypress knees jutting
from the bog in a copse of totems, and snarls
of moss fur like the bluebeards of conquistadors
or the shoulders of older gods.

Remy waits here for the apocalypse,
snaking channels sure as roads in the dark.
Manglier and mamou plants good medicine
to quell whatever ails, freshwater drum fish
a sea of sustenance below us.

We're all looking for a snake oil cure
so I gobble the lotus seeds Remy offers
in his callused palm. Like Caddo, my body
was invaded by manmade monsters
who did more killing than curing.

At dawn I go to the woods to collect spells
but am dumbstruck by the gaze of a sharp-
shinned hawk perched amid the Spanish moss
and Southern Sisters. Maybe Venus rules
Taurus, but I'm an earth dweller

praying only to gods I can taste
with my senses, sweetgum and sugarcane,
spatterdock and loblolly, clutching the cramp
in my right side like a pocketful of posies.
I'll meet Remy at the world's end

and we'll fish for our supper, brew
vats of goat weed and lizard's
tail to keep my new liver alive.
Like final girls, Caddo and I keep
crawling. We do anything to survive.

Solstice

Your aura is orange, Amara, my bruja
student declared in the days when students

talked openly before Texas tied up
their tongues. But if I cast color, surely

it's heliotrope, the violet sweep of a witch's
cape, a purple lily unfurled. Then I remember

through telescopes deep space seems draped
in black fabric, but when I smoked spirit

liana, the cosmos cradling me was not a cool
slick of midnight but a fiery sea of orange-glow

begonias, goldstone and cinnabar, calendula
and honey calcite, a potter's wheel spinning,

a curled octopus, a Carolina wren.
On this solstice I slip orange slices

into the Keepers' poppets to mimic light
on the darkest night, miniature worlds whorled

like marbled orb weavers, and in my lucid dream
I ask for winged things to ferry my ghosts to me,

expecting Ulysses, purple emperors, cobalt shocks
of blue swallowtails. Instead I see a fervor

of American copper, monarchs and buckeyes,
painted ladies peach as sweet nectar. Ballerina

moths coral my dreamscape and I bloom
like a voodoo rose. Maybe Amara knew

I'd emerge an orange queen, a ring-of-fire
daggerwing swaggering from the mud, a cluster

of crocosmia lucifers, little fallen angels
flaming to life in my hands.

POEMS FOR MY LIVER DONOR

Wish

I wish you finches,
Ruby-throated, day-lilied
cities of bitter

sunflowers, oxblood
gloves turned wrong-side out, rose
madder marrow and

velvet cake. I wish
love's thumb curved into the pink
of your spine, a bone

corset silked with red
lace. Lava rivers fever
and thrum, every

night I burn with wish.
I wish you a scarlet king-
snake, a crimson sea-

scape, radio waves
beaming cosmonaut red, your
sun a sour cherry

candying the chalk-
board black sky, your torchlit heart
a dragonfruit, dark

smudge of dahlias
smoldering on your shoulder.
My blaring June, I

wish you bright blooms, a
flame-tipped geranium, dreams
dappling your deep red

planet, and most of
all I wish you blood that plums
again and again.

Necromancy

The Moon finds the boy's body in a bag stitched
from bulls' bladders

rattling the tree where he hid as a child. It thumps
out, rock-heavy,

a sack of pipes still warm as a pudding skin. She
cradles it to

her brittle ribs, the calf of her limbs, clutching
his awkward bag

of bones, half-lunatic, half-grave. And oh, how strange
she seems

with her parceled treasure, her eyes like bits of carnival glass
mimicking the sea.

She coquets, his resting nook, his elaborate sarcophagus.
She takes

pleasure in his skin puckered and brown as figs and covers
them both in silk

the color of eggs, all myth mapped on this sapling, this jewel
on the throat

of the crone Moon silvering her clefts, bright poppet,
lucent prince.

Bright Star

When the anesthesia wanes I claw through cuffed
wrists, my glutted throat a moat of gravel, tubes
sprawling from my veins like the roots of a black
gum tree until I'm pulled back under, and I take a night
train to a half-world half a world away, a serenade
of cyanide on the bedside, a red star carved at the edge
of the Black Sea. The whittled rattle of spokes on tracks,
maps and gestures little reliquaries, a stranger's mouth
on mine, an utter hush washed over us as the lacquered
leaves of her eyes gleam greengold and my pulse rustles
like a hiss of waves. I'm dreaming my donor's dreams.
What lags behind flickers and hums. Bright star: his
mythologies nestled deep as a swell of bees in my ribs.

Iris

After the storm she moves in mourning
colors, a merger of ether and water, her father
a river god, her sisters bright birds, her hair
a cluster of bellflowers bruising the outer sky.
The ancient ones milked lilac ink from starfish,
but *her* purple ripples from a compound of coal
tar and quinine, its elusive hue marbling Victorian
Gotham in an urban sprawl, her pitcher of Styx
water pooling you into slumber heavy with plums
and mulberries, music swooning from Hell's
Kitchen all through the evening. She's a lily
of the Nile, a splendid sunbird splitting the city-
scape. She'll drag her skirts over your grave,
so please hitch a ride, my love, graze the gauze
of her moss and gossamer gown, her purple
jasper crinolines curling in rapid fronds. Charon
could ferry you through the muck and the mire,
but my money's on the goddess, flanked by violet-
backed starlings thimbling the oiled puddles,
their feathers a rainbow lattice-work, all color
refracted on the atlas of their wings. You will not be
what you were, my love, the rain transforms the water.
Riding with Iris, you're a ghost town of organza.
Flying with Iris, you're a galaxy of lace.

Black Swan

Take this waltz into the Shadowlands
where you'll know me by the hole
in my gut, the spot they carved for you.
You'll know me by the bloodflowers
budding in my gnarled garden: tuberose,
devil's trumpet, night-blooming jasmine.
We'll cheat death, pack a picnic of poppy
seeds and star-anise, all the foods that ink
the tongue, our plot lush with larks
and black-magic hollyhocks, blue
morphos and black-witch moths to quell
the shellshocks I've summoned you for.
You'll sprout vines in me, a night-phlox
spreading its fingers, lacquer seaming
the cracks with gold, and let my love
shroud you like a mourning cloak
trawling its train in the sea.

Love Letter to L

I found you at the end of hell, my lark,
my lunar eclipse, my new liver a gift
you wrapped in vellum riddled with

cellular recall, the sound of your language
doubling in my middle like bells trilling,

the seal of your cattle-prod scar on my belly
a perennial lily reflected back to me
in the glass. On the L train you illumine

the line between Brooklyn and Chelsea,
your long limbs lit up with love lies

bleeding. In French class you were everything
to me, the spoiled boys hissing *Elle* at a gazelle
in a jungleful of lions. But I knew if I let you

go, blooms would boom in me, flowers
exploding into bombs, and what I had

managed to salvage would turn savage,
curled fists opening like wild dogs
unleashed. Now, when I lose you, I simply

click my tongue to the roof of my mouth
and you roll from my lips in one long

lucent *la*. In the Garden your old soul
thrilled through Lilith, too filled with life
for Adam, and obedient Eve had no need

for you, but I do. You're in my blood. You
begin me. I'll follow you all of my life.

Harbor

Jagged birds ransack the sky, rasping
its cracks like bolt-cutters, your hairpins
caught in a tailspin, eyes burning bright

as pendants or paper lanterns. This disease,
they tell you, is too much madness, a tango
of gibbous-moon music, rain-pelts

stabbing your calves. Let my body harbor
you while the sky scrolls in circles like family
secrets or cheap souvenirs. Always

your eyes are tornadoes and brimstone,
a pine-needle fairground of fever
and gold. Again and again

the world ends, still you table your wet
boots and lilacs, black-haired as a blood-
buzz bonita dragging the wildwood inside.

Ruby

Jeegarha mani is Persian for *you are my liver*,
giver of a rush of love so crimson it floods

the bones. In Bai, the liver is an abode
of ardor, but in the West it's a laboratory

looming through subterranean tunnels
all flickers and witchfire, Victor's workshop

of filthy creation. Cardiocentric, we consider
the heart a hub, blood's currency urged

by its whooshing thump. We exchange lace-
paper valentines pink as furred tongues.

But what if we honored Elmo, saint
of sailors and livers, his luminous plasma

sparking ship masts, casting an eerie glow
in red skies at night? Instead of heart-

shaped cards, we'd swap mushroom caps,
newsboys, figure eights tipped on their sides

like looping symbols of infinity. I wonder
about the dead organ I relinquished, its bitter

antics, its swollen lobes bilious and liquorice-
black or shrunken, guttered of blood, ghost

white and lily-livered. The earliest word
for liver was *iecur*, the soulseat where fire

that flames into the brain finds its pile
of kindling, then *ficatum*, *figado*, *foie de gras*,

the plump hepatic delicacy of a fig-stuffed
goose. If our fortune is mapped on our entrails,

hieroglyphics for a haruspex to divine, then what
new language must I learn to navigate

this shimmering river? My radiant donor's fate
stenciled over my own, his liver a blood-red

beauty, a star ruby glinting like a treasure
the dragon of my ragged body hoards.

How to Describe the Sky

Say it blues like a child playing hide-
and-seek in the chiffarobe after a hush silkens
the crawlspace, after a hush ices her blood

and she reckons *no one is coming*, her finger-
tips shivering along the furs. It blues
like morning glories, their white throats

opening in September. It blues like an electric
gecko hiding from collectors, her rare brood
slinking along the screwpines in Tanzania, ribboning

the forest with trills of turquoise. It blues
like a stillness that moves. It blues like a shining
honey-creeper, her birdsong a wet whip limning

the green. It blues like folds of Veronica's velvet
unfurling in the attic, food for grizzled skipper
moths, bluing their darting tongues. It blues

like moonstone, mystical, opalescent, a gleam so brutal
it breaks your heart and feasts on its ruby pieces.
It blues like a cobalt planet raining molten glass.

It blues like a sea anemone, tentacles lulling prey
to a rapture of lapis lazuli. It blues like the Mississippi
reclaiming her Orpheus, her kingdom for a kiss

upon his shoulder. It blues like broken bottles
glinting bright as giants. It blues like a triptych
in the Rothko Chapel, each canvas bleeding

darker as his oils saturate from sapphire to slate
and the artist recoils into madness. It blues
like a bruise. It blues like my father's eulogy, a daughter

and son expunged like a crime scene scrubbed clean. It blues
like the Caribbean cradling Buck Island, the way my love
and I dove from the boat to swim through it, a roiling

remedy stripping our maladies bare. It blues like a disease
and then it quickens like the cure for it. It blues
like music, like the only hue we've got in all this darkness.

Endnote:

This collection was deeply influenced by the musical artists who shaped me, most notably The Cure, as well as:

Broken Bells
David Bowie
Jeff Buckley
David Byrne
Neko Case
Leonard Cohen
Gregory Alan Isakov
Stevie Nicks
The Pretenders
R.E.M.
and St. Vincent

Acknowledgements

My gratitude to the editors of the following publications in which these poems first appeared:

Bloodletter: "Mute"
Crow and Cross Keys: "They Ask Why You Don't Just Leave"
Driftwood Press: "Necromancy"
Hermeneutic Chaos Press: "Martial Art," "Spindle, My Spindle"
Infection House: "Ostara," "Storm Shelter," "True Crime"
Ink and Marrow: "Trail Turns Cold"
Jelly Bucket: "Hurricane Season," "Spellcraft"
Livina Press: "Ritual"
Missouri Review: "Wish"
NOVUS: "All Hallow's"
Oyster River Pages: "Bright Star"
Rockvale Review: "The Girl Without Hands," "Hungry Ghost"
Sand Hills: "2004"
Sonic Boom: "Save Me from What I Want"
Sunspot Lit: "How to Describe the Sky," "Origin Story"
Superpresent: "Malachite," "Midsummer, Oregon Coast"
Willawaw Journal: "Bolivar Ferry," "Brood 22"
Winged Penny Review: "David Bowie Is," "Iris"

About LeeAnn Olivier

Raised in Louisiana on new-wave music, horror films, and Grimm fairy tales, LeeAnn Olivier is a neo-Southern-Gothic poet. She has an MFA in Creative Writing from the University of Texas at El Paso, and her poetry has appeared in dozens of literary journals, including most recently *The Missouri Review, Bloodletter*, and *Superpresent.* She is an assistant professor of English and Humanities at Tarrant County College in Fort Worth, Texas. As a survivor of breast cancer and an emergency liver transplant, Olivier hopes to help her students navigate their own challenges through creative expression.

www.ingramcontent.com/pod-product-compliance
Lightning Source LLC
LaVergne TN
LVHW051019080826
845145LV00009B/2704

* 9 7 8 1 9 4 9 5 4 0 6 3 5 *